J. Charles Savery

Hastings and St. Leonards-on-Sea

Anatiposi

J. Charles Savery

Hastings and St. Leonards-on-Sea

Reprint of the original.

1st Edition 2023 | ISBN: 978-3-38230-536-9

Anatiposi Verlag is an imprint of Outlook Verlagsgesellschaft mbH.

Verlag (Publisher): Outlook Verlag GmbH, Zeilweg 44, 60439 Frankfurt, Deutschland
Vertretungsberechtigt (Authorized to represent): E. Roepke, Zeilweg 44, 60439 Frankfurt, Deutschland
Druck (Print): Books on Demand GmbH, In de Tarpen 42, 22848 Norderstedt, Deutschland

HASTINGS

AND

ST. LEONARDS-ON-SEA,

THEIR

𝔐eteorology and 𝔈limate:

BEING DEDUCTIONS FROM THE LAST THIRTEEN
YEARS' OBSERVATIONS TAKEN
BY Mr. BANKS.

BY

J. CHARLES SAVERY, M.R.C.S., L.S.A.,

SURGEON TO THE HASTINGS DISPENSARY, LATE HOUSE-SURGEON TO
THE NORTHAMPTON GENERAL INFIRMARY; FORMERLY ASSISTANT
MEDICAL OFFICER TO THE GLOUCESTER COUNTY HOSPITAL
FOR THE INSANE, HOUSE-SURGEON TO THE KENT
OPHTHALMIC HOSPITAL.
CORRESPONDING FELLOW OF THE MEDICAL SOCIETY OF LONDON.

LONDON:

J. CHURCHILL, NEW BURLINGTON-STREET;

W. DIPLOCK, HASTINGS;

C. H. SOUTHALL, St. LEONARDS.

MDCCCLIX.

CONTENTS.

ILLUSTRATIONS.

CHART OF THE PREVAILING WINDS AT HASTINGS
DURING EACH MONTH OF THE YEAR.

CHART OF THE MEAN DAILY RANGE OF THERMO-
METER AT HASTINGS AS COMPARED WITH
MONTPELIER AND LONDON.

CHAPTER I.

Prefatory.

I HAVE been much struck, for several years, with the misconceptions which generally exist as to the climate of Hastings, more especially in regard to the excessive heat of its summer; and I had determined that, when I had obtained a sufficient quantity of evidence, I would lay the results of my observations before the public. This was looming dimly in the distance—for I should not have been satisfied with less than six or seven years observations—when Mr. Banks, of Hastings, kindly placed at my disposal his observations, extending over a period of thirteen years. This mass of observations has remained hitherto untouched: they have been weekly published in the local papers; but no

B

"means" worked out, or any results obtained. This
has been my task in the following pages.

To those who know Mr. Banks and his famili-
arity with the use of scientific instruments, his
name will be a sufficient guarantee for the truthful
record of the readings. I have carefully compared
the instruments with which the observations of the
last few years have been made, and find they vary
very little from the Kew standard.

For the hygrometrical results, which unfortunately do not extend over more than two years, I
am indebted to Mr. Gant ; and were observed by
him at the Literary Institution. Although over so
short a period, they will give some idea as to the
moisture of the place ; and in future years more
correct (because more extensive) data will be available for the purpose.

As to the arrangement :—I have first endeavoured to give the stranger to Hastings some
general idea of its situation, with such statements
connected with its hygiene as may, I trust, prove
useful to the physician wishing to decide on

a fitting situation for an invalid. I have thought
a slight glance at its geology of sufficient interest
to devote a few lines to it. The consideration of
the climate of each month will, I hope, enable some
opinion to be formed of the weather likely to be met
with ; and the *resumé* of the meteorological results
will be of interest to the scientific observer. I
have also added a few observations on the adaptability of the climate to the several diseases for
which change of air is usually recommended ; and
trust I have been able to avoid that Charybdis of
writers on climate who fancy their own crow must
be the fairest.

I have stated, as fairly as possible, the results
at my command; and I think the great period
over which they extend will secure them from
error. It must, however, be borne in mind that
"means" deduced from no matter what number
of observations, will not agree implicitly with
any one year. They, however, serve as the best
guide at our command to the knowledge of the
climate at the particular time and place ; and it is
but reasonable to conclude that the same class of
results will be met with in future years.

The Gloucester readings, which were commenced by myself seven years ago, have been furnished me by Dr. Williams, who has continued them to the present time ; to whom, as well as to Mr. Banks, I am much indebted for their observations.

CHAPTER II.

Topographical and Hygienic.

THE sister towns of Hastings and St. Leonards
are situated on the sea coast of Sussex, nearly
south-east of London. The ridge of hills running
through the centre of the county, here approaches
the sea, and divides into several spurs enclosing
valleys, in four of which the towns in question are
placed. The valleys have mainly a southern
aspect ; and are covered, to a greater or less extent,
by houses, which are connected by rows parallel to
the sea-board, and situated under the cliff-like
terminations of the hills.

Towards the middle of the last century, when
change of climate, as a remedy for phthisis, became
more recognized, several spots in England were
selected, on account of their sheltered situation, as
localities for the winter residence of invalids.

Among these Hastings stood pre-eminent on account of its convenient distance from London, and great mildness of climate. The first of these advantages has been swept from it by the power of steam. It is not much nearer now in time than some other places. It will be my endeavour to shew to what extent its climatic advantages are still enjoyed by it.

The towns may be divided, for medical purposes, into old Hastings (comprising the Hastings valley), and those parts lying to the east of the Crescent; Hastings from the Crescent to the Infirmary, comprising the St. Mary's valley; and St. Leonards, including the valley of St. Mary Magdalen and that of St. Leonards proper.

OLD HASTINGS is that part of the town which obtained the celebrity for the locality as a winter residence for invalids. It is divided into two parts, one occupying the Hastings valley, and the other placed at right angles to it. That portion occupying the Hastings valley is defended by the east and west hills from their respective winds; while the range of hills behind protect it, to a great extent, from any wind coming from the north : the only winds to which it is exposed, therefore, are those from the south-east to south-south-west. The western portion of Old Hastings is absolutely protected from all northerly winds, but is more exposed to those blowing due east or west and round by the south.

Let us examine, in succession, a few localities in this division. *High Wickham*, situated on the east hill, is one hundred and eighty feet above the sea, facing W.S.W. It is much exposed to the south-west winds, but defended by the hill, which rises one hundred and thirty feet above it, from the east and south-east winds. It is a fine, bracing summer residence. *The main streets* are absolutely *sheltered from all winds* but the due south, which sweeps through them. The *Croft, Gloucester-place, Church-street*, are slightly exposed to the south-east wind ; but defended by the hill from the south-west, west, and north winds. *George-street* is defended from nearly every wind except a gale from the south-west. The *Parade* and *Pelham-place* are defended from all winds north of south-west and east ; and are open to the sea, and therefore exposed to all winds blowing over it. They face nearly due south.

HASTINGS, though not so protected on the whole as the old part of the town, presents many spots nearly equally well suited for the abode of the invalid. It may be likened to an inverted ⊥, including the St. Mary's valley and the prolongations, east and west, to meet Old Hastings and St. Leonards. That portion going eastwards, including *Pelham-crescent* and *Breed's-place*, faces nearly south ; and, being placed beneath the Castle cliff, is defended by it from all winds north of west and east, but is exposed to the full influence of the south-west breezes. The *St. Mary's valley* has a mean direction from north-west to south, and is much exposed to the northern blasts ; but the eastern part, under the Castle Hill, is protected by it from all winds to the east of north and south. This portion includes *Wellington Square, Castle Hill, Spring-terrace,* and *St. Andrew's-terrace. St. Mary's-terrace,* also in this division (one hundred and ninety feet above the sea), participates in the same advantages as High Wickham. It has a south-west aspect, defended by the hill from the north-east ; and in summer is a bracing situation. Proceeding westwards, *York Buildings* is defended by the houses behind from the northern winds. *Robertson-street* is principally occupied by shops. *Caroline-place* and the houses adjacent have much the same aspect as Breed's-place ; but the cliff not being so near, they have more air. *Carlisle-parade* and *Robertson-terrace* are protected by Robertson-street from the north. They have a south-south-west aspect, and extend across the St. Mary's valley, in front of the sea. They are by far the finest houses at present in Hastings. *White Rock-place* lies beneath the hill : it has a south-east aspect, facing the sea, and is defended by the hill from all winds north of south-west and north-east.

ST. LEONARDS, in a climatic point of view, may be divided into three parts—1. The sea-line from the Infirmary to the Colonnade ; 2. The Magdalen Valley ; and 3. The portion of the town west of the Colonnade. The first portion includes *Verulam Place, Eversfield Place, Grand Parade,* and a portion of the *Marina.* The aspect of this division is south-south-west ; it lies beneath the hills, which have been cut away for its reception; and is by them defended from all winds north of west and north-east, but is exposed to the full influence of the winds south of these points. Its proximity to the parades and beach offers great advantages in point of air and exercise. The *Magdalen Valley* has a direction nearly parallel to that of St. Mary's, and is at present much exposed; but, as buildings progress, this will be obviated to a great extent. The third division of St. Leonards, that portion west of the Colonnade, has a directly south-west aspect, and is much exposed to the westerly winds south of north-west; but it is defended by the cliff and upper part of the St. Leonards valley from all winds north of north-west round to east-south-east. *Maze Hill* and the *Undercliff* are defended from all northerly and easterly winds. The upper parts of St. Leonards, *West Hill* and the *Uplands,* are more bracing.

I have thus endeavoured to give a *coup-d'œil* of the various localities in the towns; but this sketch would not be useful in a medical point of view, did I not also mention a few points in relation to its hygiene, of vast importance to any proposing to resort thither. These points are, its drainage, water supply, and, most important of all, its facilities for exercise.

Formerly there was an impression that the towns were badly drained,—and certainly the rumour had some foundation ; but, since the establishment of a Board of Health, the system has undergone a complete revision, and now there are few towns in the kingdom in which the drainage system is better ; and, provision having been made for its increasing population, there is no reason to fear any recurrence of the complaint.

The towns are supplied with water from several sources. The geological formation, owing to the absence of extensive beds of clay, is not favourable for the development of considerable springs : much of the supply is, therefore, dependent on the more shallow springs which derive their existence from the rain-fall on the neighbouring hills. The five principal sources are : (1), the reservoirs in the Ecclesbourne valley, which communicate, by means of a tunnel, with (2) the reservoirs in the upper part of the Hastings valley, which are placed near a

tolerably constant spring. In the St. Mary's valley
are (3) the borings near the gas-works, lately
undertaken by the Local Board of Health, and
which have already reached the depth of 350 feet;
and (4) the Eversfield waterworks, which supply
the western part of Hastings and the eastern division of St. Leonards; while the central and western
portions of St. Leonards are supplied by (5) a
spring situated beneath the sandcliff, and driven
by steam thence into covered reservoirs for the
service of the town.

In quality the water itself is good; but after a
heavy, long-continued rain is apt to be rather dis-
turbed. Circumstances have lately led to its being
submitted to Professor Taylor, of Guy's Hospital,
for analysis; and he thus states his opinion of its
quality : "The specimens resemble pure, soft water
derived from beds of sand. They are colourless,
and without taste or smell; for the most part
bright and clear, depositing but a small amount of
siliceous matter. The mineral constituents are
sulphate and carbonate of lime, chloride of sodium,
carbonic acid, and air." Besides the water supplied
by the companies, there are also several other

springs which feed the town pumps, and which are also generally very pure.

Situated on the West Hill, St. Leonards, is a spring containing a sufficient amount of iron to be available in those diseases for which chalybeate waters are usually employed. This spring has been enclosed, and is now known as the St. Leonards Spa. There are also several other sources which contain a certain amount of iron; but none in which the quantity is so great, nor their situation so convenient, as this.

As regards facilities for exercise, the invalid may find on the parades a promenade unrivalled in extent in the United Kingdom, consisting of nearly two miles of gravel walk, always dry, and defended from the northerly winds. The parades face the sea, and, by their proximity to the road, afford a constantly varying scene to occupy the mind. Should he be stronger, and able to take more extensive walks, those in the neighbourhood are very varied, and present numerous peeps of lovely country. Romantic glens, ruined castles, and old churches, are sufficiently accessible to amuse the

lover of the picturesque and the antiquary. The
formation presents many attractions to the geolo-
gist; the ferns and plants to the botanist; whilst
the microscopist can find an endless source of
amusement in the pools of the seashore and the
ditches near Bulverhythe; the artist has often enriched his canvas with the scenes on the beach;
and, in fact, there are few amusements which cannot be profitably followed here by those whose
strength enables them to pursue them.

CHAPTER III.

Geological.

ANY attempt to go deeply into the geology of this portion of Sussex would be obviously misplaced in a work of this character; but it is necessary to obtain some idea of the formation on which the towns are situated, so that its effect on the climate may be appreciated. It will also, I trust, furnish a few hints as to the position in which the strata of the neighbourhood are to be found by those of our visitors whose attention has been turned in this direction. The towns are situated in the centre of the Wealden formation, whose geology has been so much enriched by the labours of Dr. Mantell, to whose works, and those of Dr. Filton, I am indebted for this sketch.

The Wealden formation took place in the earliest part of the cretaceous age, following closely upon

the Portland beds of the Jurassic series : it consists
of four divisions—the lowest or Purbeck beds, the
Ashburnham clays, the Hastings sands, and the
Wealden clay. The Jurassic series contain principally remains of a marine origin ; whilst, in the
Wealden formation, the remains are exclusively of
land animals and plants. In the immediate neighbourhood of Hastings, these strata can be very
conveniently examined at the East Cliff, where the
Tilgate beds, rich in fossil remains, occupy the
upper part ; below this, the Hastings sands are developed to a considerable extent ; while the lower
seventy feet are composed of strata of shales, clays,
and sandstones, rich in iron and vegetable remains,
which constitute the Ashburnham beds. The principal mass of rocks being composed of sand, they
easily absorb any amount of rain, and prevent any
evil effects which might happen from so large a rain-
fall as is incident to a marine situation. As now
constituted—the greater part of the towns being
on sand, the rest on shingle, a still more pervious
substance—no sooner does the rain cease than the
ground becomes almost immediately dry, and the invalid is able to take exercise with safety. The Hastings sands form the great forest ridge of the Wealden,

which extends for many miles along the coast, from Bexhill to beyond Rye; it gradually rises from its point of appearance; and its upper strata can be more conveniently studied near Bulverhythe than at the East Cliff, although their *relations* to the other members of the group cannot be so well seen; it rises until it approaches Cliff End, about four miles east of Hastings; and thence, having attained the point of dip, the strata gradually subside, the lower portion of the series only being developed in Pett level. The adjacent formations are most easily observed to the westward. The Wealden clay appears at Bexhill, and bends round to Hollington, where deposits containing "paludinæ" are found; the clay, in its turn, is overlaid by the higher members of the Cretaceous group; the Greensand appears at Pevensey, which is then covered by the Gault,— this, however, is scarcely perceptible during low water at Sea-side houses near Eastbourne,—and it has again above it the upper Greensand and Chalk of Beachy Head. The same alternation of strata can be traced eastward near Folkestone, and northward at Tonbridge.

The fossil remains of this period are very rich

(about two hundred animal genera being found)
and interesting, from the presence in them of a
large number which do not appear in any other
formation. Two birds and five reptiles of large
size are peculiar to these strata. The Iguanodon
Hylæosaurus, Pelosaurus, Megalosaurus, Crocodiles
and Chelonians, Pterodactyles, Fishes, Insects, Fresh-
water molluscs and crustaceans, Conifers, Cycadeæ,
and Ferns, will repay the labours of the successful
investigator.

It is clear that the land must have formed a
portion of the delta of a large river, or of a vast
fresh-water lake, to allow of the deposition of the
quantities of land animals and plants which are
found buried in its rocks; the whole formation
must then have been violently upheaved at a time
corresponding to the forest ridge of the Wealden,
and the upper members of the group were then removed by water forming the valleys of denudation
in which the towns are built.

CHAPTER IV.

The Months.

JANUARY.

Barometer.—The mean pressure is 29·80. The range of this month, with March and November, is the greatest during the year, viz., 1·01. The mercury has once stood at 30·53, and once at 29·11, during the past thirteen years.

Thermometer.—The mean thermometer reading, during the last ten years, has been 38°.3, which exceeds that of Greenwich by 2°.6. The variations from this normal mean are very small; and the mean daily range is but 8°.3. The range at Gloucester is about 11°, and in London 9°. In 1857, when the reading at Gloucester was 12°, at Hastings it was 21°—one of the coldest points recorded.

Wind.—The wind in this month presents great

variations in different years, which principally occur in the relative proportions of the north and south-west winds, both having in different years ranged as high as 18 days; the average for the last thirteen years being—for the south-west, 10; and north, 6·4 days. Next in frequency are the south and north-east, which blow each 3 days; east, south-east, and west, blow 2 days; and north-west, 1·7. The proportions of the latter winds are tolerably constant.

Weather.—Nine days may be expected in which rain falls. Of these, nearly all have some portion of the day fine; the proportion of wet days being 0·7. The mean amount of rain for the month is 2·35 inches.

FEBRUARY.

Barometer.—The mean of the month is 29·84. The mean range, ·96. The highest reading in thirteen years was noticed in this month, viz. 30·70 in 1847.

Thermometer.—The mean differs little from that

of Greenwich: it is 38°.7. But its mean daily range is 9°.2; that of London being 12°. The mean monthly readings rarely vary more than 3° from the average. The previous history of this month affords us an instance of the equability of this climate when other parts of England are suffering from extremes. During the great cold of 1855 we of course experienced a depression of temperature; but, while at Uckfield the thermometer sunk to 11°, at Gloucester to 5°, and in London to zero, the lowest point attained here was 15°; and the mean daily range of the month did not vary from the average. This is the lowest reading recorded at Hastings during the past thirteen years.

Wind.—The north and south-west winds have each nearly the same mean reading, being 7·7 and 8 respectively. But they vary widely in different years. In 1854 the north blew 15 days; and in 1848, the south-west 18. The north-east and east are also variable in the different years, the means being 2·4 and 3·1; while the west and north-west are more constant to 2 and 2·4.

Weather.—The mean amount of rain is 1·58,

being the least of any month in the year. The quantity, however, varies a good deal in different years. The days on which rain falls are 5·5 ; the proportion of 0·7 being still continued for all-day rain. The fine, clear days are about thirteen : a number which varies little in succeeding years.

MARCH.

Barometer.—The mean pressure, 29·81. The range is the highest mean in the year, viz. 1·02. The yearly means are very variable.

Thermometer.—The mean temperature of March is 39°.6, which is slightly below that of Greenwich for the same month ; but the mean range of the month is 10°.7, which shews that the variations are much less than those experienced inland,—the range for London being 14°; and in 1857 the mean range at Gloucester exceeded the range here by 5°. The lowest point attained in this month has been 23°, in 1850 ; while at Gloucester the *highest* mini-mum is 24°.

Wind.—The north, north-east, and east winds have much increased in frequency, and blow about the same number of days of each, viz. 6, 5, and 5·5. The south-west has diminished to 6·4, but is more constant. The west is very constant to the extent of 3·2 days. The south and south-east scarcely blow at all in this month.

Weather.—The mean quantity of rain is still low, being 1·70. The rainy days are 6·8; but six of these are either fine, or overcast, half the day. The fine, clear days are fourteen.

APRIL.

Barometer.—From this month to July the mean range diminishes gradually. This month it is ·72. The mean atmospheric pressure is 29·84.

Thermometer.—The mean of this month is identical with that of Greenwich, viz. 45°.7. The mean daily range is 11°.9; that of London being 19°.

Wind.—The north and north-east continue to

predominate this month to the extent of 6·3, 4·8, and 4·4 days respectively. The south-west has increased in frequency, its mean number of days being 8·7. The south and south-east are very low in amount ; but the south wind usually blows one day in each year.

Weather.—The rain has a mean of 2·48 inches ; and the rainy days attain the number of 7·8, being a slight increase on last month. The proportion of whole day's rain is, however, very small, several years occurring without one. The fine days are twenty-two, of which sixteen may be reckoned as fine and clear.

MAY.

Barometer.—Mean is rather low, 29·79 ; the mean range, ·72.

Thermometer.—The readings now begin to assume their summer aspect, and to read lower than Greenwich. The mean here is 51°.7, that of Greenwich being 1° higher. The range also has not much increased, while that of London is still 19°. This is also the case at Gloucester. The lowest readings rarely approach the freezing point here, whilst at other places they have not disappeared from the annual register until next month.

Wind.—As we approach the summer season, we find the south-west wind beginning to assert its preeminence. In this month it has an average of 10·4, and is very constant. Next in frequency is found the east, 6·5 ; north, 4·3 ; and north-east, 4, which have somewhat diminished from the earlier months. The south and south-east are rather more frequent ; whilst the north-west and west are sensibly diminished.

Weather.—The rain presents much variety, none falling in 1848, and nearly 4·00 in. in 1856. The mean number of rainy days is 6·5 ; but ten years have occurred without one day of steady rain. The fine, clear days are 16·2 ; and the fine days on which rain fell, 4·5.

JUNE.

Barometer.—Mean pressure, 29·84. Mean monthly range, ·64.

Thermometer.—The greatest thermometric range, 14°.9, is attained here this month; the corresponding range for London being 20°; at Gloucester, 23°. The mean is precisely the same as at Greenwich, viz. 58°; and the variations from the mean temperature are very small in different years.

Wind.—The south-west wind is still the prevailing breeze; it blowing 14 days on an average, and is very constant in its numbers, more so than in any other month. Next in frequency, but more variable, is east, 4·6; whilst the north and north-east, which are tolerably regular, have each a mean of 2·7. The order of succession below this, is, west, north-west, south, and south-east.

Weather.—The mean fall of rain is 1·85; and this amount is remarkably regular, only in 1852 has it varied much from the average. The fine, clear days have greatly increased in number, being 18·5; whilst a thoroughly rainy day may be expected once in two years.

JULY.

Barometer.—The mean pressure for this month is 29·85, rather above the average. The column is steadier than in any other month. Its range has not exceeded 1·01 for twelve years; and its mean range is ·61.

Thermometer.—Here, as at other places, we have the highest mean temperature in this month : it is 59°.7, being 1°.6 below the mean of Greenwich. The mean daily range, however, begins to decrease, it being 13°.6; that of London being still 19°. The highest temperature is recorded in this month, viz. 95°, in 1854 ; in other years it has rarely exceeded 82°.

Wind.—The south-west wind, which has been increasing the last few months, attains its maximum now, viz. 15·2. It therefore blows nearly half the days of the month. The most constant wind is the west, which blows 3·3 days; whilst the north, north-east, and east, maintaining their relative frequency, vary much in different years.

Weather.—The fine, clear days are 18·4 ; and

the fine days on which rain falls, 4·1. We may
assume the number of fine days to be twenty-eight,
as those on which merely a shower fell are classed
as fine rainy days. The fine days are also remarkably constant in their number. The mean amount
of rain is 1·97 in. ; but its quantity varies much
in succeeding years.

AUGUST.

Barometer.—Mean, 29·88. The mean monthly
range is increasing, being ·66, but is still very
steady.

Thermometer.—The temperature of this month
is still below the mean reading of Greenwich, it
being 59°.4, though its variations from the mean
are rather more than in other months. Its mean
daily range is small, 12°.3, when compared with
London, which is 18°. The same range is found
at Gloucester.

Wind.—The most prominent feature in the wind

of this month is the decline of the south-west from its maximum, its frequency being only 12·2; whilst the north has increased much both in frequency and regularity in different years, and now numbers 4·8 days. The next wind in number is the east, 3·4 days; which is nearly balanced by the west, 3·2. The north-west and north-east have also the same numbers, 2·5.

Weather.—The mean amount of rain is 2·86 in. The number of fine, clear days has attained its maximum, 19·6; and if to these are added the fine-cloudy, and fine-rainy days, the number is increased to twenty-seven days of sunshine: a number which is very constant in the different years.

SEPTEMBER.

Barometer.—The mean attains its maximum, viz. 29·91. The mean range is .85.

Thermometer.—The mean temperature of the month is 55°.2; the cooling influence of the sea still maintains its power, it being 1°.1 lower than the Greenwich mean. Its range is 11°.6, being 6° less than that of London.

Wind.—The characteristic feature of this month is the absence of a prominent wind. The south-west has withdrawn to 7; while the east, north, and west, have all increased to nearly the same. The north is most constant; the east, which is always found, varies from 1 to 15 days, its mean number being 6.

Weather.—The peculiarity of the month is the extreme regularity of its fine-clear days, viz. nineteen. In twelve years it has not departed more than two days from the average, and three years only have varied so much as that. The days on which rain falls are 5·1, of which three are fine-rainy days.

OCTOBER.

Barometer.—Mean, 29·75, but varies much in different years. The mean range is ·95. The lowest readings in the thirteen years occurred in this month, viz. 28·89 in 1852.

Thermometer.—The mean reading for this month is 50°.3, being 1° *above* that of Greenwich. The means are remarkably constant; and the daily range is small, viz. 10°.3, the corresponding ranges at London and Gloucester being 15° and 12°. The thermometer occasionally touches the freezing point in this month, viz. one year in four. It does so nearly always elsewhere.

Wind.—The winds of August and October are remarkably similar; the principal variation being that the north is more frequent, having increased to 7, at the expense of the north-east and south-east winds.

Weather.—We may expect a rainy day in this and each of the two following months, the weather becoming more overcast; but the fine-clear days still number twelve, and twelve more may be accounted fine. The rain attains its highest point in this month, viz. 4·44, and the rainy days are 8·5.

NOVEMBER.

Barometer.—Mean, 29·81. The range has been steadily increasing since July, and now amounts to 1·00 : hence, on the whole, it gradually declines.

Thermometer.—The mean temperature is 42°.8. The minimum thermometer usually falls to a degree or two below 32° in this month ; but not nearly so much as in other localities. Another instructive instance of the equability of the climate occurs in the weather of last November. At Gloucester the mercury sank to 18°.5; near London, to 15°; whilst here the minimum attained was 31°; and the mean daily range of the month was as nearly as possible the average. The daily range is 9°.3, that of London being 11°, and Gloucester 12°.

Wind.—A great change has taken place in the average direction of the wind, which has now taken on its winter type ; and the north wind asserts its pre-eminence. It blows to the extent of 11 days, the south-west having declined to 6·6 days. The north and north-east have the same frequency, viz. 2·8 ; the former, however, being the most constant. The south-east, west, and north-west, are all diminished to 1·5.

Weather.—The fine-clear days maintain their number, 12·5 ; and about 13 more may be called fine, though the proportion of cloudy days has increased to 6·5. The number of rainy days has fallen to 7·5. The mean quantity of rain is 2·63. Fog rarely occurs in this month.

DECEMBER.

Barometer.—Mean pressure, 29·84 ; mean range, ·93.

Thermometer.—The mean of this month is 41°.2, nearly 3° above the Greenwich mean ; but its main feature is an extremely small daily range, its mean being only 7°.7, that of London being 10°. The lowest temperature recorded in this month is 17°, to which the thermometer descended in 1855, the corresponding day at Gloucester being 11°.

D

Wind.—The wind retains the type of last month, the only prominent difference being the increase of the west wind at the expense of the north-east.

Weather. The dry days of this month are 23·4, of which twelve are fine and clear. The mean amount of rain is 2·19 ; that of rainy days, 7·6.

CHAPTER V.

The Instruments.

BAROMETER.

But little information on the climate can be obtained from the mean barometric readings, its indications being more valuable in its daily than in its monthly alterations. The mean pressure, deduced from thirteen years daily observations, is 29·83 ; and we find that no month varies more than ·08 from this mean, while ten months do not vary more than ·04. The monthly range diminishes from November, when its range is 1·00, with considerable regularity, to July, when it is ·61, again increasing to November. The mean range is, however, considerably less than at Gloucester, although the same law of progression is observed there. Taking the mean monthly range of Hastings at ·84, the range at Gloucester is 1·16; the extremes being

1·47 and ·68. This peculiarity of the barometer readings here was noticed by Sir James Clarke in his work on Climate; and in his tables Hastings has a lower annual range than any other English climate, viz. 1·56.* They, however, are only founded on three years observations; and the more extensive series at my command places the mean annual range at 1·36, being a little above that of Rome and Malta, and below that of Florence. The maximum readings observed in the different months in any year, shew a curious monthly progression. The highest recorded in any July is 30·25; in August, 30·35; September, 30·43; October, 30·45; November, 30·58. The maxima are then not so regular until March, which has 30·63; April, 30·42; May, 30·37; and June, 30·33.

THERMOMETER.

The thermometric indications do not differ so greatly from Greenwich in point of position in the

* The Sanative Influence of Climate, by Sir James Clarke. Table VII. Churchill.

scale, as in their greater uniformity and freedom
from extreme changes. The mean of the year is
48°.3, identical with that of Greenwich; but in
winter the temperature is warmer, and through the
summer uniformly colder, than at that place. The
thermometer is lower than Greenwich from March
to September, and above it from September to
March.

The peculiar position and soil of the towns secure
them from those great changes which so seriously
affect the rest of England. Of course these changes
are perceived here, but not nearly to such an extent
as elsewhere. The great cold of 1855 only carried
the thermometer down to 15°, while at London it
was at zero. And the great and sudden vicissi-
tudes experienced in November 1858 were hardly
appreciable here; the mean range of the month,
from my own observations, being only 9°.2. This
exemption from great changes would lead us to
expect a small daily range; and such we find to
exist, the range being less than at most places on
the South Coast. This, and its freedom from the
great alterations of the rest of England, renders it
a peculiarly suitable climate for the pulmonary in-

valid. During the winter months the range is
only 8°.5 ; and though during the summer it considerably exceeds this, yet it is very much less than
at London and other inland places. The annual
range is 58°.3, being less than that of Montpellier,
Pau, Nice, or Rome.*

THE VANE.

The most frequent wind is the *south-west*, which
blows 116·8 days in the year. It is most frequent
in July, when it blows 15 days. In September it
has fallen to 7 ; where it remains almost stationary
until it attains its minimum in March, viz. 6·4.
From this it steadily increases in frequency to July.

North.—The north wind has 74·5 days, and is
very regular in its course, attaining its maximum
in November, 11 ; and then sinking gradually to
July, 2·6, whence it again increases.

East.—The east wind is next in order of frequency, viz. 46. It also is tolerably regular in its

* Sir J. Clarke, op. cit.

course, attaining its maximum in May, 6·5, and decreasing to December and January, whose average number of days is 2.

North-east.—This wind blows 38 days. Its rate of increase from its minimum in October, 1·7, to its maximum in March, 5, is very regular: its decrease is also steady.

West.—The west wind has 32·7 days on an average. It is more irregular than the previous winds; but it appears to have its greatest frequency in September.

North-west.—Blows about 21·8 days. It has two maxima, March and August, 2·5; whilst in May and November it has sunk to its minima.

South.—This wind blows on an average 18 days in the year: its course is tolerably regular from a maximum in January to a minimum in July.

South-east.—The south-east is the least frequent and most irregular of all the winds. It blows only 15 days.

I have appended a set of diagrams of the wind for each month, in which the foregoing results are depicted in such a way as to render the progress of each wind in the different months apparent to the eye. If the reader supposes the lines E W to represent the towns in each figure, and the position of the hills behind them be remembered, he will have some idea of the mode in which they are affected by the wind in each month.

THE RAIN-GAUGE.

The mean quantity of rain which falls here is 28·87 inches. This is greater than that of London by 4 inches; but is not more than might be expected from its proximity to the sea, and is about the same as that of Madeira. The tables on which the calculations have been based, unfortunately, do not present the rainy days with sufficient accuracy to deduce from them the mean of each month; but from a careful review of them, and comparison with other data, I am induced to place the annual number of days on which rain can be registered at

135. This small number of days, the few thoroughly rainy days, and the high rain-fall, would lead us to conclude that the rain, when it does fall, is very heavy ; and this we find to be the case. In seven years there were one hundred and sixty readings above 0·40 in., of which eighteen were above 1 inch in the twenty-four hours. But the soil, sloping position, and drainage, prevent any evil effect from the large downfal ; and half-an-hour after a heavy shower, the streets and parades are sufficiently dry for exercise.

THE WEATHER.

Before stating the results I have evolved respecting the weather, I must detail the mode in which they have been deduced. For thirteen years Mr. Banks has recorded it twice, and for the last five years, four times a day. A day which is registered as fine, morning and evening, is termed a "fine" day ; one in which cloudy is registered at one or the other time, is termed "fine-cloudy"; and one entirely overcast, "cloudy." The days on which rain was registered once, and fine once, including showery days, are "fine-rain." These may therefore all be classed as fine days, in the ordinary acceptation of the term. The "cloudy-rain" have one registry, "overcast"; and those in which rain is registered at all times are termed "rainy."

The whole number of fine days is 189. They advance with great regularity from their minimum in January to their maximum in July, and then as steadily decrease. The "cloudy-fine" days number 46; the "cloudy", 52; the "fine-rain", 42; and the "cloudy-rain", 30·5; while the "rainy" days only amount to 9 in the year. From this it is evident that the number of days on which the invalid cannot get out, on account of the weather, is very few; and those on which he may enjoy the rays of the sun, so conducive to health and vigour, are 280. To these must be added 52, which are dry though overcast; hence there are 332 days in which a person may enjoy a walk. The regularity of these results, and the small amount of variation year after year, is very remarkable, and has much surprised me, as the fickleness of the weather in England has passed into a proverb.

THE HYGROMETER.

Our knowledge of the moisture of Hastings is at present in a very unsatisfactory state; but it appears, during the two years under notice (1856 and 1857), that the humidity was in excess of the average Greenwich mean; but I find as observations multiply, so the results get gradually nearer. In January, of four years observations the mean is scarcely above that of Greenwich; and in December, three years results give a less mean. The mean of the winter months, from November to February, have only one degree of humidity more than Greenwich; the excess being at present in the summer months, where increased observations may still reduce the variation.

CHAPTER VI.

The Climate.

IN considering the climate of the towns of Hastings and St Leonards in relation to disease generally, we must class it among those climates of an unstimulating character which are termed "relaxing". It is to this character that it owes its adaptability to the cases of Phthisis, Dyspepsia, and Bronchitis, which are so much benefited by it. But it is only on the hale, strong, and robust, that it exerts any relaxing influence; while its very relaxing power is that which renders it so genial to the feelings of the invalid. It is not relaxing to them: on the contrary, there are some cases for which it is too stimulating, and for which the more decidedly relaxing climates of South Devon and the Undercliff must be prescribed. It must also be borne in mind that the peculiar climate is only found beneath the hills; *upon* them we have a bracing air closely resembling that on the Yorkshire coast, as appears from the observations conducted by Mr. Rock at Fairlight; and between these points nearly every gradation of climate may be found.

As to differences of temperature in different parts of the towns below the hills, there are at present no sufficient data on which to ground an opinion. A society, however, is now in existence for comparing the meteorological readings at several stations; and in a year or two it is to be hoped that reliable facts may be accumulated, which will determine the various conflicting opinions now in circulation. It is, however, evident that certain situations are much more defended from the colder winds than others; and it therefore follows that these are more peculiarly suitable for those cases of phthisis which require protection in the winter months. These most sheltered spots are to be found in the Old Hastings Valley, where scarcely any wind from a cold quarter penetrates. George-street, the Parade, Pelham-crescent, Breed's-place, Wellington-square, and the houses close beneath the Castle Hill, are all sheltered from the prevailing winter winds. The same advantages are also enjoyed by the Undercliff, and the lower part of Maze Hill and The Ascents, in St. Leonards.

Those invalids who are able to take more exercise, and to brave the south-westerly winds, may find a more congenial abode in those situations facing the sea, which are defended from the northerly winds. The sea-line of St. Leonards and Hastings, as far as Breed's-place, offers admirable residences for the bronchitic and dyspeptic invalid, and their proximity to the parades presents great facilities for exercise. While those persons who require a more bracing air may find it at High Wickham, St. Mary's-terrace, St. Michael's, in Hastings; or at the West Hill, or Uplands, in St. Leonards.

Phthisis.—In regard to the climate adapted to the treatment and residence of persons suffering from pulmonary consumption, Dr. Francis observes:[*] "The good which it is reasonable to expect may be effected by a judiciously chosen climate, in this disease, is to improve that state of fading health

* Change of Climate, by J. T. Francis, M.D., page 3. Churchill, London.

which, generally speaking, precedes and marks the
approach of the lung affection ; to arrest the development of tubercle when it has already commenced ; and, by avoiding much of the risk which
exists in a cold, damp air, of contracting local in-
flammation of the lung or bronchial tubes ; and, in
cases of chronic phthisis, the prospect which a
favourable atmosphere affords of protracting more
or less indefinitely the progress of the complaint.—
It must, however, be borne in mind that *the*
remedy which, above all others, is useful in the
early period of phthisis, is the opportunity of
breathing fresh air without risk of taking cold ;
—not for one only, but for many hours daily."

The climate of the towns may be thus viewed
under two aspects as regards the pulmonary invalid: first, as a permanent residence ; and, secondly,
as a resort during the winter months. As a permanent residence, it presents many advantages.
The temperature is not warmer, but the extremes
are less, than in other parts of England. The
climate is not *so* relaxing as other points on the
South Coast ; and the facilities for exercise (the
great point for the invalid in every period of the

year) are unrivalled. Its easy distance from the
metropolis is an advantage to those whose relations
are resident there ; while the beauty of the neighbouring scenery, and its many resources for quiet
enjoyment, render it a spot where, the first seeds of
this scourge of English society being arrested, a
restoration to strength may be looked for with
hope.

"Doubtless," Dr. Francis observes,* "the most
hopeful prospect which change of climate holds out,
occurs in young persons in that state of cachexia
which immediately precedes the development of
tubercle. There are few cases in which this stage
of warning is not present"; and "it is at this
period that the hope, approaching to a certainty,
may be held out, that, by a residence for a time in
a more favourable climate, the constitution will be
enabled to fortify itself against the attack by which
it is threatened." These remarks apply with great
force to a residence in our own climate, where the
small range of the thermometer—only one degree
above that of Rome—and the very small barometric range ; its sheltered situation from the nor-

* Op. cit., p. 43.

thern winds ; its sandy soil, retaining the heat and moderating the cold, which affect other places not so favourably situated ; all combine to render it one of the most favourable spots for a permanent residence for one in whom consumption is threatened.

But it is as a winter residence for the invalid that Hastings has justly acquired such renown. To it resort those for whom the South of Devon is too relaxing, and who find beneath its warm hills that shelter from the northern blasts which is so necessary for their comfort and safety during this period of the year. It is not so much that the temperature is warmer,—though that exercises a great influence on the well-being of the patient,— as that the mean daily range is very small. (Temperature viewed alone gives a very faint idea of the value of a climate for an invalid's residence. The variations are of *infinitely* greater importance : as an example, Berlin and Edinburgh have the same annual mean ; but the winter at Berlin is 10° colder, and the summer 10° hotter, than at Edinburgh.*) It is the great equability of the climate that has

* Physical Atlas, by Keith Johnston.

rendered these towns so peculiarly favourable for a
winter sojourn. It is better that the patient should
arrive at the middle of October, as by that means
he will avoid the prejudicial effects of the November fogs, which are almost unknown here. During
ten years, "fog" has only been registered seven
times in this month; and in only one did it receive
more than a passing note on the register. On the
contrary, the mean of thirteen years shews that
nearly twenty days of sunshine may be expected;
and the month so ungenial elsewhere, is by no
means so at these towns. His stay may be advan-
tageously prolonged into March; the hills affording
him more shelter from the northern winds than
can be found in most other places; and the temperature elsewhere has not yet sufficiently assumed
its Spring aspect to warrant the risk of exposure
to the north-east winds in a colder climate. In
fact, in April we find the cold is often down to the
freezing point at other stations, which is unusual
here in that month.

Dyspepsia receives much benefit from the air of
these towns, in those cases in which it has been
properly selected. No climate is good for all forms

of the disease ; and it is, to a great extent, owing
to a want of judgment in the selection of cases
that so much disappointment is experienced from
change of air. Adopting that truly practical division of Sir James Clarke, into inflammatory, atonic,
and nervous, it is in the last variety that most
benefit is to be expected from this climate. The
general *malaise* and irritability, weight and sense
of vacuity of the stomach, chilliness and headache,
often vanish after a short residence in this locality.
The inflammatory form often complicates this variety ; and in this the more sheltered parts of the
town are preferable ; but for the purely gastric
affection the climate is not sufficiently relaxing,
and that of South Devon or Spain is more useful.

Bronchitis.—The air coming into direct contact
with the lining membrane of the air-passages is
more apt to produce functional changes in it than
in those other mucous membranes which are not
so immediately exposed to its influence ; and we
accordingly find that bronchitis is, of all others, the
disease which most speedily yields to change of air.
A patient having an undue sensitiveness of the
membrane, suffers much on the occurrence of cold,

irritating winds; whilst those in which the general
condition is one of atony, also experience much in-
convenience if the naturally abundant secretion is
increased by great changes of temperature. These
varieties require different climates for their treatment; and in the irritable form there are few
localities which can compare with that of these
towns, while the more sheltered spots *on the hills*
are well fitted for the residence of those in whom
a more copious expectoration is the type of the
disease. Many persons suffering habitually from
winter cough, lose it entirely while resident in this
locality.

Taken as a whole, these towns are remarkably
healthy, as appears from a late report of the Regis-
trar-General, in which Hastings ranks among the
highest of healthy places. This opinion was derived from the reports of deaths; and therefore
requires some amount of correction, as the number
of deaths of persons not belonging to the town are
included in the return; and the census, upon which
the data are grounded, was taken at a time when
the towns were remarkably empty. Either of these
causes would tend to raise the proportion of the

mortality; and if they could be satisfactorily removed from the calculation, it would probably be found that the towns were the most healthy spots in England; enjoying an equable climate,—no noxious trades being carried on; having a sufficient amount of ventilation, good drainage, and water. Few places can be cited in which all these advantages are found; and we accordingly find that, although the strumous diathesis is very prevalent among the lower classes, from improper food and other depressing causes, still it rarely passes into the more aggravated form of phthisis.

STATIONS

OF THE

Hastings and St. Leonards Meteorological Society.

FAIRLIGHT . . .	MR. J. ROCK, JUN.
HIGH WICKHAM . .	MR. E. FIELD.
HIGH-STREET . . .	MR. R. DUKE.
GEORGE-STREET . .	MR. GANT.
BLEAK HOUSE . . .	MR. BANKS.
PRIORY HOUSES . .	MR. PENHALL.
MARINA, ST. LEONARDS .	MR. CHAS. SAVERY.

Explanation of Diagrams.

I.—Shews the Prevailing Winds for each month in the year, from thirteen years' observations. The distance from the centre of the circle to the apex of each cone, measured *from* the point from which the wind blows, and compared with the scale, will indicate the mean number of days on which each wind may be anticipated.

    Example. NOVEMBER.—North, 11; north-east, 2·8; east, 2·9; south-east, 1·6; south, 2·2; south-west, 6·6; west, 1·6; north-west, 1·3.

II.—Shews the mean Daily Range of the Thermometer for each month in the year, as compared with Montpelier and London.

    Example. APRIL.—Hastings, 11·9; Montpelier, 14; London, 19

PREVAILING WINDS

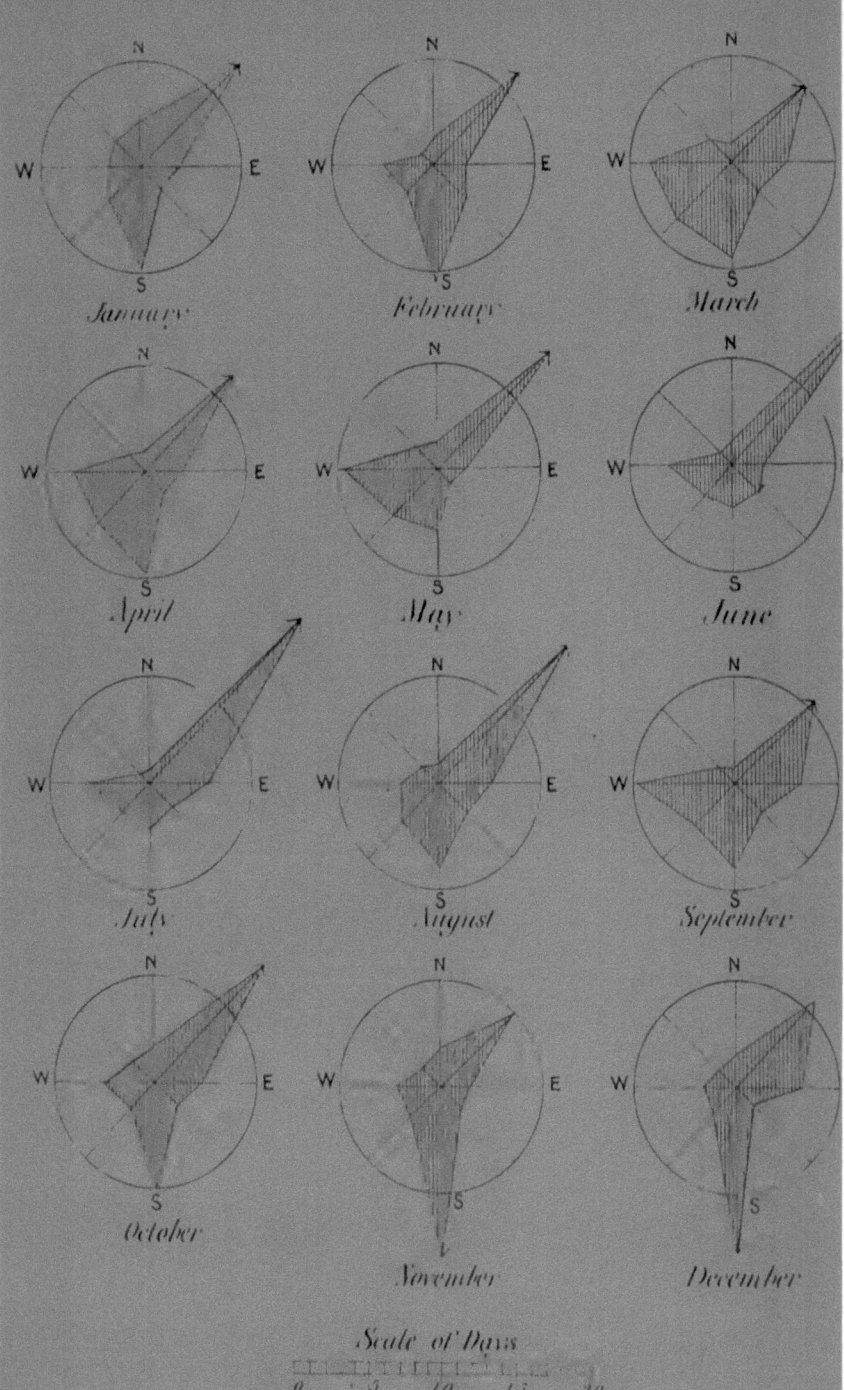

January February March

April May June

July August September

October November December

Scale of Days
0   5   10   15   20

MEAN DAILY RANGE OF THERMOMETER

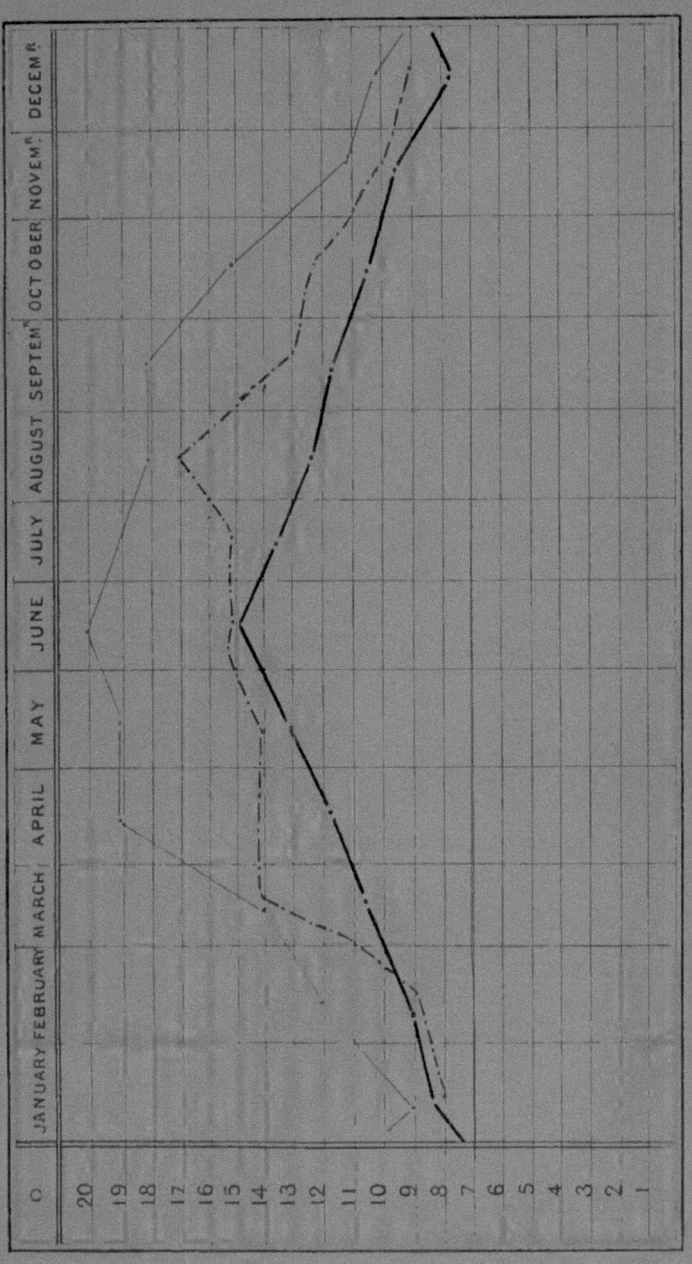

Hastings ———   _Environs of London_ ———   _Montpelier_ —·—·—·—